J

Main

FAMOUS ATHLETES

LEBRON JAMES

by Tracy Nelson Maurer

Gail Saunders-Smith, PhD, Consulting Editor

Pebble® Plus

CAPSTONE PRESS
a capstone imprint

Pebble Plus is published by Capstone Press,
1710 Roe Crest Drive, North Mankato, Minnesota 56003
www.capstonepub.com

Library of Congress Cataloging-in-Publication Data
Maurer, Tracy, 1965–
    LeBron James / by Tracy Nelson Maurer.
        pages cm.—(Pebble plus. Famous athletes)
    Includes bibliographical references and index.
    ISBN 978-1-4914-6236-2 (library binding : alk. paper)—ISBN 978-1-4914-6252-2 (ebook pdf)—
ISBN 978-1-4914-6256-0 (pebble books pbk. : alk. paper)
1. James, LeBron—Juvenile literature. 2. Basketball players—United States—Juvenile
literature. 3. African American basketball players—Juvenile literature. I. Title.
    GV884.J36M39 2016
    796.323092—dc23
    [B]   2015001867

Editorial Credits
Erika L. Shores, editor; Juliette Peters, designer; Eric Gohl, media researcher;
Lori Barbeau, production specialist

Photo Credits
AP Photo: Tony Dejak, cover; Newscom: Icon SMI/Bob Falcetti, 9, KRT/Ed Suba Jr., 11, 13, KRT/
Phil Masturzo, 7, Reuters/Mike Blake, 15, Reuters/Mike Ehrmann, 17, Reuters/Mike Segar, 19,
USA Today Sports/David Richard, 1, 5, 21, 22

Design Elements: Shutterstock

Note to Parents and Teachers

The Famous Athletes set supports national curriculum standards for social studies related to people, places, and culture. This book describes and illustrates LeBron James. The images support early readers in understanding the text. The repetition of words and phrases helps early readers learn new words. This book also introduces early readers to subject-specific vocabulary words, which are defined in the Glossary section. Early readers may need assistance to read some words and to use the Table of Contents, Glossary, Read More, Internet Sites, Critical Thinking Using the Common Core, and Index sections of the book.

Printed in the United States of America in North Mankato, Minnesota.
052016   009763R

TABLE OF CONTENTS

LOVING THE GAME

LeBron Raymone James has
always loved basketball. He was
born December 30, 1984.
Even as a baby, LeBron played
with a toy basketball every day.

1984

born in
Akron, Ohio

4

LeBron's mother, Gloria, raised

him by herself. They moved often.

LeBron almost quit sports after

fourth grade. Then in 1994

a coach asked LeBron to live

with his family in Akron, Ohio.

born in
Akron, Ohio

lives with the
Frank Walker
family for
the next
two years

HIGH SCHOOL STAR

By 10th grade LeBron was
6 feet, 7 inches (2 meters) tall.
He stood out as a star
on his high school football
and basketball teams.

1984

born in
Akron, Ohio

1994

lives with the
Frank Walker
family for
the next
two years

1999–2003

attends
St. Vincent–
St. Mary
High School

9

LeBron made great shots.

He passed the basketball well.

LeBron ruled the court.

Fans called him "King James."

1984

1994

1999–
2003

born in
Akron, Ohio

lives with the
Frank Walker
family for
the next
two years

attends
St. Vincent–
St. Mary
High School

NBA SUPERSTAR

After high school LeBron was the top pick in the 2003 NBA Draft. The Cleveland Cavaliers chose him. LeBron was happy. He would play for his home state's team.

NBA stands for National Basketball Association.

 1984
born in Akron, Ohio

 1994
lives with the Frank Walker family for the next two years

 1999–2003
attends St. Vincent– St. Mary High School

 2003
drafted by the Cleveland Cavaliers

13

The Cavaliers became

a better team with LeBron.

He helped them win

more games than

in past seasons.

1984

1994

1999–
2003

2003

born in
Akron, Ohio

lives with the
Frank Walker
family for
the next
two years

attends
St. Vincent–
St. Mary
High School

drafted
by the
Cleveland
Cavaliers

After seven years,

the Cavaliers still had not

won a NBA championship.

LeBron left Cleveland to play

for the Miami Heat in Florida.

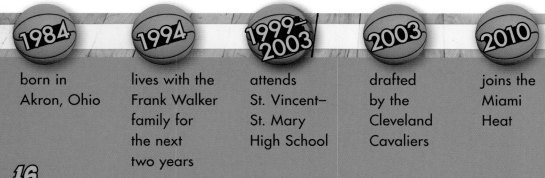

1984
born in
Akron, Ohio

1994
lives with the
Frank Walker
family for
the next
two years

1999–2003
attends
St. Vincent–
St. Mary
High School

2003
drafted
by the
Cleveland
Cavaliers

2010
joins the
Miami
Heat

LeBron and the Miami Heat
played in the NBA Finals
each year between 2011
and 2014. LeBron was named
the Finals MVP in both 2012
and 2013.

MVP stands for Most Valuable Player.

 1984
born in
Akron, Ohio

 1994
lives with the
Frank Walker
family for
the next
two years

 1999–2003
attends
St. Vincent–
St. Mary
High School

 2003
drafted
by the
Cleveland
Cavaliers

 2010
joins the
Miami
Heat

 2012–2013
Miami Heat win
back-to-back
championships

BACK HOME

LeBron returned to the
Cleveland Cavaliers in 2014.
He had a great season
playing for his home team.
LeBron led them all the way
to the NBA Finals.

1984
born in
Akron, Ohio

1994
lives with the
Frank Walker
family for
the next
two years

1999–2003
attends
St. Vincent–
St. Mary
High School

2003
drafted
by the
Cleveland
Cavaliers

2010
joins the
Miami
Heat

2012–2013
Miami Heat win
back-to-back
championships

2014
returns to the
Cleveland
Cavaliers

GLOSSARY

court—the hard surface on which a basketball game is played

draft—an event held for teams to choose new people to play for them

NBA Finals—the games that decide the season's championship

season—the time of year in which NBA basketball games are played

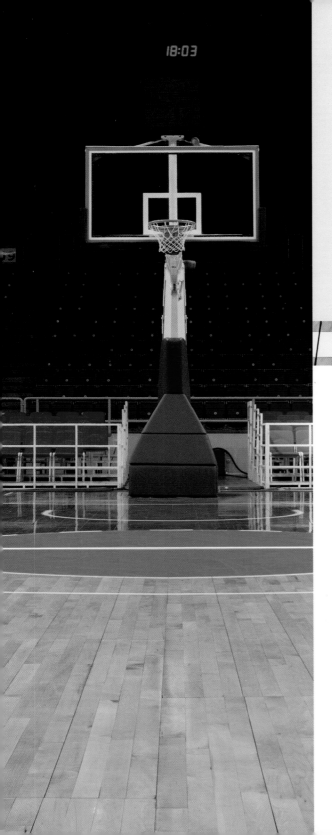

READ MORE

Ciovacco, Justine. *LeBron James: NBA Champion.* Living Legends of Sports. New York: Rosen Publishing, 2015.

Doeden, Matt. *Stars of Basketball.* Sports Stars. North Mankato, Minn.: Capstone Press, 2014.

Nagelhout, Ryan. *I Love Basketball.* My Favorite Sports. New York: Gareth Stevens Publishing, 2015.

INTERNET SITES

FactHound offers a safe, fun way to find Internet sites related to this book. All of the sites on FactHound have been researched by our staff.

Here's all you do:

Visit *www.facthound.com*

Type in this code: 9781491462362

Super-cool stuff! Check out projects, games and lots more at **www.capstonekids.com**

CRITICAL THINKING USING THE COMMON CORE

1. Why do fans call LeBron "King James"? (Key Ideas and Details)

2. What is one reason LeBron may have returned to the Cavaliers in 2014? (Integration of Knowledge and Ideas)

INDEX

Word Count: 226
Grade: 1
Early-Intervention Level: 18